Dear Parent:

Congratulations! Your child is taking the first steps on an exciting journey. The destination? Independent reading!

STEP INTO READING® will help your child get there. The program offers five steps to reading success. Each step includes fun stories and colorful art. There are also Step into Reading Sticker Books, Step into Reading Math Readers, Step into Reading Phonics Readers, Step into Reading Write-In Readers, and Step into Reading Phonics Boxed Sets—a complete literacy program with something to interest every child.

Learning to Read, Step by Step!

Ready to Read   Preschool–Kindergarten
• big type and easy words • rhyme and rhythm • picture clues
For children who know the alphabet and are eager to begin reading.

Reading with Help   Preschool–Grade 1
• basic vocabulary • short sentences • simple stories
For children who recognize familiar words and sound out new words with help.

Reading on Your Own   Grades 1–3
• engaging characters • easy-to-follow plots • popular topics
For children who are ready to read on their own.

Reading Paragraphs   Grades 2–3
• challenging vocabulary • short paragraphs • exciting stories
For newly independent readers who read simple sentences with confidence.

Ready for Chapters   Grades 2–4
• chapters • longer paragraphs • full-color art
For children who want to take the plunge into chapter books but still like colorful pictures.

STEP INTO READING® is designed to give every child a successful reading experience. The grade levels are only guides. Children can progress through the steps at their own speed, developing confidence in their reading, no matter what their grade.

Remember, a lifetime love of reading starts with a single step!

DISNEP
fairies

Pixie Hollow Tales

Step into Reading, Random House, and the Random House colophon are registered trademarks of Random House, Inc.

Visit us on the Web!
www.stepintoreading.com
www.randomhouse.com/kids

Educators and librarians, for a variety of teaching tools, visit us at
www.randomhouse.com/teachers

ISBN: 978-0-7364-2773-9
Printed in the United States of America   10 9 8 7 6 5 4 3 2 1

STEP INTO READING®

Disney fairies

Pixie Hollow Tales

Step 3 and Step 4 Books

A Collection of Four Early Readers

Random House 🏠 New York

Contents

STEP INTO READING®

STEP 3

Beck's Bunny Secret

By Tennant Redbank
Illustrated by Denise Shimabukuro
and the Disney Storybook Artists

Random House 🏠 New York

Beck looked to her right.

She looked to her left.

She looked behind her.

Then she smiled.

She was alone.

She parted the blades
in a clump of grass
and slipped inside.

Beck had a secret.

It was a very fuzzy secret.

It was a baby bunny named Bitty.

Beck was taking care of him.

"I can't let anyone
know you are here,"
Beck said to Bitty.
She stroked his soft ears.
"Especially Fawn."
Fawn always teased Beck
about her baby animals.

This wasn't the only time

Beck had helped a stray animal.

First there was the baby skunk.

P-U!

Rosetta was mad at her

for ages after that.

Then there was

the baby warty toad.

He was very cute.

But he made Beck's skin

all bumpy.

The worst was the egg

Beck found in Brackle Swamp.

She didn't know

it was a crocodile egg!

Fawn always scolded
Beck about the baby animals.
Beck didn't want
to get in trouble.
Beck stroked Bitty's soft fur.
"But you're so cute!" she said.
Suddenly, she heard a voice.

"Beck! Where are you?"

Beck gasped.

It was Fawn!

"Shhh," Beck told Bitty.

Beck flew over to Fawn.

"There you are!"

Fawn said to Beck.

Rustle, rustle, rustle.

"What's that noise?"

Fawn asked.

Beck's face turned red.

Bitty must be hopping about!

Rustle, rustle, rustle.

Fawn pointed to Bitty's hiding spot.

"It's coming from

that clump of grass!" she cried.

Beck told Fawn it was
just the wind.
Fawn shook her head.
"I'm not a weather talent,"
she said.
"But even I can tell
there's no wind today."
Fawn flew over to the grass.

Beck covered her eyes.

Fawn parted the grass
and looked inside.

Beck peeked between her fingers.

There was nothing there.

Bitty was gone!

Beck dropped her hands.

"See? It was the wind,"

she said.

Fawn shrugged.

Then she flew off.

Right away,

Beck dove into the grass.

She searched high and low.

Bitty was not there.

Bitty was missing!

Beck had to find him.

Where would a baby bunny go?

Bunnies loved to eat.

Beck flew to the gardens.

She checked the lettuce patch.

Nothing.

Beck tried the carrot patch.

All the carrots were in order.

There was no sign of Bitty.

Beck looked at the peas . . .

and the beans . . .

and the beets.

No baby bunny had nibbled them.

Beck flew to the fairy-dust mill.
"Has anything been eating
your pumpkin shells?"
she asked Terence.
Terence shook his head.

Maybe Bitty wasn't hungry.

Maybe he was thirsty!

Beck flew to the stream.

Rani was making a leaf boat.

"Have you seen

any paw prints nearby?"

Beck asked

the water-talent fairy.

"No," Rani told her.

"But if I do, I'll let you know!"

Where could Bitty be?

Beck checked

Mother Dove's nest.

She checked Tinker Bell's workshop.

She dropped by Bess's art studio.

She stopped by Lily's garden.

She couldn't find Bitty anywhere!

Beck flew to the tearoom.

Dulcie the baking-talent fairy

was in a tizzy.

"Something has been nibbling

my carrot cake!"

Dulcie cried.

She pointed at the cake.

There was a huge chunk missing

from one side.

Beck clapped her hands together.

It had to be Bitty!

She looked around.

But she didn't find

the baby bunny.

She found Prilla

with icing on her lips

and a piece of cake in her hand.

"It tastes good!"

Prilla told Beck.

Beck's wings drooped.

She flew slowly

out of the tearoom.

She had looked everywhere.

There was no sign of Bitty.

Beck sighed.

She had no choice.

She had to ask Fawn for help.

Fawn would tease her.

But together they might

find the lost baby bunny.

Beck flew to where
she had seen Fawn
earlier in the day.
Fawn wasn't there.
But then Beck heard
a familiar sound.
Rustle, rustle, rustle.
The noise was coming
from a clump of clover.

She flew closer.

Rustle, rustle, rustle.

Beck parted the leaves

of the clover.

Inside was Fawn . . .

with Bitty!

"Fawn!" Beck cried.

Fawn jumped.

Her glow turned bright pink.

"Oh, Beck! I've been taking care

of this lost baby bunny,"

Fawn said.

"I didn't want to tell you

because I always tease you

for taking in baby animals."

Beck laughed and laughed.

Fawn put her hands on her hips.

"What's so funny?"

she asked.

"I was taking care
   of the bunny, too,"
   Beck said.
"So you see,
   we kept Bitty a secret
   from each other!"

Fawn laughed, too.

Beck and Fawn linked hands

over Bitty's soft fur.

"I have an idea," Beck said.

"From now on,

let's take care of Bitty

together!"

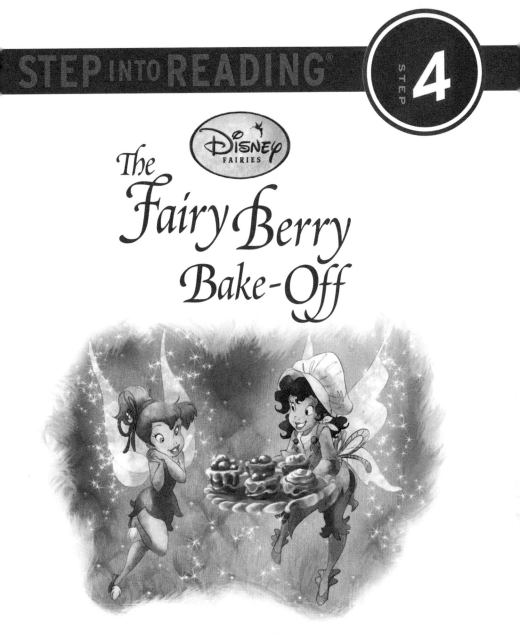

DISNEY
FAIRIES

The
*Fairy Berry
Bake-Off*

By Daisy Alberto

Illustrated by the Disney Storybook Artists

Random House 🏠 New York

All over Pixie Hollow, the Never
fairies were hard at work. Each fairy
had a talent and a special job to do.

The garden-talent fairy Lily was
in her garden, watering the seedlings.

The art-talent fairy Bess was in
her studio, working on a new
painting.

The water-talent fairy Silvermist was collecting dewdrops.

The light-talent fairy Fira was training the fireflies to light Pixie Hollow at night.

The animal-talent fairy Beck was
helping a lost baby chipmunk find
his way home.

And Tinker Bell, a pots-and-pans
fairy, was in her workshop, fixing a
broken frying pan.

But no matter how busy they were, the fairies all stopped what they were doing at lunchtime. They headed to the tearoom to eat.

The tearoom was one of the most popular places in Pixie Hollow. It was peaceful. It was pretty. And best of all, the food was yummy!

The fairies gathered there every day for all of their meals.

"I wonder what tasty treats the baking-talent fairies will have for us today," said Lily.

"Maybe we'll have whole roasted cherries with cinnamon glaze," replied Bess.

"Yum!" exclaimed Tink. "I'm so hungry, I could eat a whole cherry all by myself."

The other fairies laughed. They couldn't wait to find out what was for lunch.

Strawberry soup, nutmeg pie, blackberry cake, and roasted walnuts stuffed with figs—every fairy had a favorite dish!

There were so many wonderful
treats, Tinker Bell couldn't decide
what to try first. At that moment,
something special caught her eye.
She popped a tiny tart into her
mouth.

"That's the best tart I've ever had!"
she said.

In the kitchen, Dulcie, a baking-talent fairy, overheard Tink. "Tinker Bell loves my tarts!" she exclaimed with a smile.

Dulcie was proud of her baking. She always tried to make the fluffiest rolls, the flakiest pies, and the creamiest frosting. She really loved to bake. But she also loved to watch the other fairies enjoy her tasty treats.

The baking-talent fairy Ginger was nearby. When she heard Dulcie, she frowned.

"I think that was one of *my* tarts," she told Dulcie.

"Oh, I don't think so," Dulcie said sweetly. "Your tarts tend to be a little dry and hard."

Ginger most certainly did not agree. She knew that her tarts were always moist and flaky.

The next day, Dulcie baked
blueberries with fresh whipped
cream. The fairies ate every last one.

"Yum!" said Tink. "Are there
any more?"

Dulcie blushed. She beamed.

"They love my baking!" she said
proudly.

Dulcie wanted to be the best
baking-talent fairy in all of Pixie
Hollow.

Back in the kitchen, Dulcie peeked into the oven. She saw Ginger's gingerbread.

"It looks a little flat," she said. "You should follow my recipe, Ginger. My gingerbread is much fluffier."

Ginger had had enough of
Dulcie's bragging.

"My gingerbread is perfect,"
she said.

"No, it isn't. But don't feel bad,"
said Dulcie. "Some fairies just need
more practice than others."

That did it! Ginger was fed up.

"Dulcie, you wouldn't know what to do with a berry if it fell into your piecrust!" said Ginger.

"Ha!" said Dulcie. "I could outbake you any day!"

"Prove it," said Ginger.

"You're on!" cried Dulcie.

The fairy berry bake-off began. Ginger and Dulcie were going to prove once and for all who was the best baker. It was a battle neither fairy wanted to lose.

That evening, Ginger made boysenberry custard served in a vanilla bean. Dulcie made her magic blackberry turnovers.

"Wow!" said Tink. "They really
do turn over!"

The next day, Ginger made her famous five-berry crumble. The fairies cleaned their plates and licked every last crumb from their spoons.

Dulcie peeked into the tearoom. "Hmmph," she said. "Wait until they try *mine.*"

Dulcie carried her right-side-up upside-down cake into the tearoom and proudly placed it on a table. The fairies didn't even notice. They were too busy finishing Ginger's five-berry crumble.

Dulcie couldn't believe it.

"Don't you like my cake?" she asked the fairies.

"It looks wonderful," said Tink. "But we're full."

Dulcie frowned. "How about just a little taste?" she pleaded.

The fairies shook their heads. They patted their stomachs.

"We couldn't eat another bite," Bess said.

Ginger grinned. It looked like
she had won this round of the berry
bake-off.

Dulcie knew she needed to make something extra-special for the next meal. So for lunch the following day, she outdid herself.

There were puddings and pies. There were crumpets and cakes. There were piles of Tink's favorite cream puffs.

The fairies ate and ate until they couldn't eat any more. Dulcie's feast was a hit.

But the berry bake-off was only getting started.

The next day at breakfast, Dulcie and Ginger waited in the tearoom for the fairies to arrive.

"Try a muffin," Dulcie said to Tink. "They are soft and sweet."

"How about a honey bun?" asked Ginger. "They're even softer and sweeter."

"No, a muffin!" said Dulcie.

"A bun!" cried Ginger.

"Er, I'm not hungry," said Tink, flying away.

Dulcie and Ginger didn't even notice that Tink had left. They kept arguing.

The fairies worked hard all morning. They were looking forward to a nice, relaxing lunch. Dulcie and Ginger met them as they entered the tearoom.

Dulcie waved a spoon. "Taste this!" she called out.

"No, taste this!" shouted Ginger. "Mine's better!"

But none of the fairies stopped. The tearoom no longer seemed very relaxing at all!

Back in the kitchen, things were no better.

"Get me an egg!" Dulcie shouted to an egg-collecting fairy.

"I need more flour!" Ginger snapped at a kitchen-talent sparrow man.

One by one, the other fairies left the kitchen. They didn't want to be around Dulcie and Ginger. The berry bake-off was getting out of control.

Soon Dulcie and Ginger were
alone in the kitchen. But they didn't
notice. They were both too busy.

They sifted and stirred. They
mixed and measured. They each
wanted their next dessert
to be their best.

Ginger made fresh raspberry
cupcakes with vanilla cream filling.
She used the finest raspberries that
grew in Pixie Hollow.

Dulcie made her special seven-
layer cake, with six kinds of
berries.

Dulcie reached for a berry to top off her cake.

"That's *my* berry!" Ginger exclaimed. "You can't have it."

"It's *my* berry," Dulcie replied. "I'm sure of it."

"It's mine!" said Ginger. She grabbed the berry.

"No, it's mine!" said Dulcie. She held on tight.

Neither fairy wanted to give in. They pulled and pulled, until . . .

. . . Dulcie stumbled backward—
right into her cake!

Ginger stumbled backward, too.
Her cupcakes went flying
everywhere!

"Oops!" said both fairies at once.

One cupcake hit Dulcie. Another hit Ginger.

Just then, Tink walked in to see what all the fuss was about. A flying cupcake landed right on her head.

"Hey!" cried Tink. "What is going on here?"

Dulcie and Ginger looked
around. The kitchen was a disaster.
Cake and cupcakes were everywhere!
"Oh, no!" said Dulcie.
"What have we done?" cried
Ginger.

They rushed over to Tink.

Tink was mad. "The berry bake-off has gone too far," she said. "Don't you understand that you are both great bakers?"

Dulcie and Ginger blushed. They looked at each other. Could it be true? Could they *both* be great bakers?

Dulcie brushed Ginger's cupcake crumbs off her apron. She tasted her fingers.

"Oh, my," said Dulcie. "This is good!"

"Really?" asked Ginger.

"Yes!" said Dulcie.

Ginger smiled. She took a tiny taste of Dulcie's seven-layer cake.

"Wow," she said. "So is yours!"

"Why don't you bake together?" Tink suggested.

And so the fairy berry bake-off
ended in a tasty tie.

Disney fairies

A Game of Hide-and-Seek

By Tennant Redbank

Illustrated by the Disney Storybook Artists

Random House New York

Pixie Hollow was quiet and still.

No fairy wings fluttered.

No fairy voices filled the air.

Where had all the fairies gone?

Suddenly,

along came Tinker Bell.

She flew alone

over a garden.

Tink pulled up close

to a tall tulip.

Rosetta peeked out
from behind some petals.
They were playing a game
of fairy hide-and-seek.
And Tinker Bell was IT!

Tinker Bell still had
so many fairies to find.
There were Rani and Bess,
Nettle and Fira,
Dulcie and Terence,
Silvermist, Iridessa, and Fawn.
Beck was usually easy to spot.
She couldn't stay still for long.
But Prilla was very good
at hide-and-seek.
It might take Tink a while
to find her.

Tinker Bell looked behind
a spiderweb.

She checked under a pinecone.

She peeked into a knothole.

Then she saw a bright light.
It was shining from
behind a leaf.

Only one fairy glowed

that brightly.

"Fira!" Tink yelled.

Tink pulled the leaf back.

There she was!

"You found me!"

Fira said, giggling.

Tink couldn't stay to talk.

She had other fairies to find!

Tink flew over the meadow.

She stopped short.

She sniffed the air.

She smelled lemons.

Tink followed her nose . . .

right to Dulcie,

a baking-talent fairy.

Dulcie was hiding

near a patch of clover.

The lemon cake she had baked

that morning gave her away!

Tink left the meadow
and started searching again.
Bright blue footprints
crossed her path.
The footprints led
over some pebbles
and down to the river.
There Tink saw Bess
hiding among the pussy willows.

"How did you find me?"
Bess asked.

Tink pointed to the
art-talent fairy's feet.
The bottoms of her shoes
were covered in blue paint!

"Oh, drat!" Bess exclaimed.

"I spilled some paint
in my room today.
I must have stepped in it!"

Tink found Silvermist
behind a rainspout.

She spotted Fawn
in a bird's nest.

Iridessa was trying to blend in
with the fireflies.

Nettle was hiding
in an old cocoon.

Tinker Bell still had not found
all her friends.
She flew to the Mermaid Lagoon.
There she saw water flowing
from a large stone
sitting on dry ground.

Tink fluttered around the stone.

On the other side,

she found Rani,

a water-talent fairy.

Rani was playing

with a water ball.

"I got you!" Tink shouted.

Rani jumped.

She was startled.

She dropped the water ball.

It burst into a hundred droplets.

Then Rani pulled all the drops
back together again.

She threw the water ball at Tink.

Tink sprang out of the way.

"Hey!" Tink yelled.

"We're playing hide-and-seek,
not fairy tag!"

Tink had a game to finish,

so she flew into the woods.

"I can't believe

I haven't found Beck," she said.

Up ahead, she saw

a flash of color.

Tink flew closer.

It was a red-spotted toadstool.

But wait . . .

something was behind it.

Maybe it was Beck!

It wasn't Beck.

But it was a

red-haired fairy in a green cap.

"Prilla!" Tink shouted.

Tink told Prilla

who she had already found.

Then Prilla cried out,

"Tink, look!"

A beetle floated

right in front of their noses—

upside down!

It sparkled with fairy dust.

Tink and Prilla followed
the trail of fairy dust.
Fairy dust makes
fairies fly—and beetles, too!
They flew until they saw
a silly sight.
Terence, a fairy-dust-talent
sparrow man,
was trying
to pull beetles
from the air.

"Tink, Prilla, help!"

Terence cried.

"I was hiding in a little hole.

A bunch of beetles found me and

got into my bag of fairy dust!"

Prilla stayed to help Terence.

Tink still had more fairies to find.

Who was left?

Tink settled on a lily pad

to think for a bit.

She had found Terence and Prilla,

Fawn, Iridessa, Rosetta,

Nettle and Silvermist,

Dulcie, Rani, Fira, and Bess.

The only fairy

she had not found was . . .

Beck!

Tink flew off again.

She looked and looked.

Then she asked

the other fairies for help.

They all joined in.

They explored every garden.

They searched over the meadow

and the lagoon

and the fairy-dust mill.

Where in Pixie Hollow was Beck?

Tink tugged at her bangs.
She was stumped!
Beck was usually
the easiest fairy to find.
Today Beck was not just
an animal-talent fairy—
she was a master hider!

Tink was about to yell
"Come on out, Beck!"
But before she did,
a soft sound reached her ears.
It seemed like a breath.
Or a whisper.
Or . . . a snore!

Tink followed the noise.

It was coming from a hollow log.

She poked her head inside.

There she found

Beck curled up

with a family of hedgehogs!

"Wake up, sleepyhead!" Tink sang out.

Beck opened her eyes and yawned.

"You found me already?"

Beck asked.

"Already?" Tink cried.

"I've been looking for hours!

Beck, you are the last

hide-and-seek fairy!"

"I am?" Beck asked.

"How nice!"

She rolled over.

She snuggled back in

with the hedgehogs.

Soon Beck was asleep again.

Tink sighed.

Beck and the hedgehogs

looked so cozy.

Tink pushed Beck over a little.

She was tired after

all that looking.

Maybe a little nap . . .

only for a minute or two . . .

Just before Tink's eyes closed,

she heard a voice call,

"Tink? Beck?

Where are you?"

Another game of

fairy hide-and-seek had begun!

Disney fairies

Pixie Hollow Paint Day

By Tennant Redbank

Illustrated by the Disney Storybook Artists

Random House New York

Bess was an art-talent fairy. She was working on an important painting. She had been painting day and night for almost two weeks. It hadn't been easy. She was having trouble getting the picture just right. But now she was almost done.

Bess held a bottle up to the light. It looked empty. She turned it upside down. A single drop of blue paint slid out.

"Oh, polka dots! I'm out of blue paint!" she wailed.

Bess thought for a minute.

She grabbed a tube of purple paint.

She squeezed it flat. Only a tiny bit

came out.

"Oh, no! I'm out of purple, too!" Bess

groaned. She needed to get more.

Bess went over to her paint shelf. There was no blue or purple paint. The red paint was almost gone. She'd left the lid off the yellow paint and it had dried up. And the only green paint she had was lime green.

Bess put her hands on her hips. There was just one thing to do. "It's time for a paint party!" she declared.

Making paint by herself was a lonely task. But making paint with other fairies was fun!

Bess sent invitations to her friends. She asked Tinker Bell, Rani, Beck, Fawn, Lily, Prilla, Silvermist, Fira, and Rosetta. None of them were art-talent fairies. Still, everyone said yes—everyone except Rosetta.

When she got the invitation, Rosetta
went to see Bess. "Paint making?" Rosetta
said. "That sounds messy." She didn't like
getting dirty!

Bess shrugged. She had plenty
of help.

Bright and early on a sunny morning,
the fairies gathered in the meadow.

"Reporting for paint duty!" Tink said.
She gave Bess a little salute.
"Point me to the paint pots!"

Bess laughed. "Not yet," she said. "First we have to find some colors." Bess told her friends that paint was made from plants and flowers and other things found in nature. The fairies could find what they needed all over Pixie Hollow.

Bess had made a list for each fairy. It told them what to look for.

The fairies were eager to begin. Lily
knew right away where to find the
buttercups and sunflowers for the
yellow paint—in her own garden! She
picked a huge armful of both.

Tink flew into the forest. She was
looking for pine needles. They made the
best dark green paint.

Prilla picked a patch of violets.
They would make a lovely shade of
purple paint.

Rani filled an entire basket with
raspberries and cherries. Bess could use
them to make the perfect red paint.

Silvermist was in charge of the orange paint. She carefully dusted the wings of an orange butterfly. A little butterfly dust went a long way!

Blueberries were great for blue paint.
And Fawn and Beck knew of a huge
blueberry bush where their bird friends
always went to eat.

White paint came from chalky
pebbles deep in caves. Bess sent Fira to
find those. The light-talent fairy used
her glow to light the way.

Meanwhile, Bess set up a row of coconut shells in the meadow.

One by one, the fairies came back with their finds.

"Put the blueberries in that shell over there," Bess told Fawn and Beck.

"What lovely violets!" Bess said
to Prilla.

"Those sunflowers and buttercups
will make such bright paint!" she gushed
to Lily.

Each fairy put what she had found into one of the coconut shells. Bess added some linseed oil to each shell. This would help turn each item into paint. Then the fairies stepped into the shells and started to stomp!

Fawn stomped on the blueberries. "Oooh, the berry mash is oozing into my shoes!" Fawn cried.

"You should try the pine needles," Tink said. "They tickle my feet!" She lifted up a pine-green foot to show everyone.

"This is hard! I want to eat the raspberries," Rani said. "They smell so good!"

Fira was working on the white paint. She smashed the pebbles with Tink's hammer. Then she mixed the bits with the linseed oil.

Kindhearted Lily couldn't bear to crush her sunflowers and buttercups. She turned them over to Prilla. Lily worked on the purple paint instead.

"You are all doing such a great job!" Bess said. "This is going to help me so much with my painting!"

The fairies kept stomping and crushing and mixing and churning. Their feet were all sorts of bright colors. And they were having a good time.

"Tell us about your painting, Bess," Silvermist said.

Bess thought for a moment. "Well, it's a big picture of the Home Tree in late-afternoon sunshine. The painting has a golden glow." She paused. "I like it, but something's missing."

Bess had an idea. "I know!" she said. "I'll show you my painting! Maybe you can help!" She flew out of the meadow.

A few minutes later, Bess was back.
In her hands was a large painting. She
leaned it against a tall flower stem.

The fairies crowded around to look at Bess's painting. It was very pretty. But Bess was right. Something was missing.

"Maybe some of this new paint will help," Prilla said. She always looked on the bright side.

"Maybe," Bess said. Then she sighed and gave her friends a smile. "I know what I want to do. I don't want to work on this painting right now. Let's put away all this beautiful paint!"

The fairies quickly began to bottle the paint. All of a sudden, they heard a noise. It came from just outside the meadow.

"What was that?" Tink asked. The fairies heard twigs cracking. They heard leaves crunching. They heard . . . *RIBBET!*

A giant frog leaped into the clearing!

"Strongjump!" Fawn cried.

Strongjump was Fawn's frog friend.

He heard her call and launched himself at her.

"Strongjump, no!" Fawn shouted.

It was too late. Strongjump landed
right in the coconut cup of red paint.
It splattered all over!

From there he made another mighty
leap—straight into the green paint.
Splash! Green paint sprayed the meadow.

"Wait, Strongjump!" Fawn yelled.

But Strongjump didn't want to wait. He hopped into the orange paint and the white paint and the blue paint. He overturned the purple paint. He knocked over the yellow paint.

Paint splattered everywhere!

Fawn flew right up to Strongjump.
She came nose to nose with him. "Stop!"
she yelled. He stopped.

"Good frog," Fawn said. She patted
him on the head.

"It's my fault," Fawn said to the other fairies. "I told Strongjump I would play with him today. Then I forgot. He came looking for me. He was so happy to see me that he didn't watch where he was going."

"That's okay," Bess said. "A little paint never hurt anyone!"

The fairies looked at themselves. A little paint? Hardly! They were covered head to toe with every color.

Prilla giggled. There was paint in
their hair. Paint on their clothes. Their
legs were colored up to their knees. And
they had paint on their cheeks, noses,
elbows, and ears.

The other fairies began to smile.
They put their arms around each other.
Then they laughed until their sides hurt.

Then something caught Lily's eye.
"Oh, Bess!" she cried. "Your painting!"

The fairies all turned to look at
Bess's painting. It had been splashed
with paint, too! Streaks of red and
orange and green and yellow crossed the
canvas. White spots and blue splotches
dotted the Home Tree. A big blob of
purple filled one corner.

Bess flew over to the painting. She
was very quiet. The other fairies watched
her. They didn't know what to say.

Bess looked at the painting up close. Then she backed up and looked at it from far away. She studied it from the left and from the right.

Slowly, a smile spread across her face. She turned around.

"I like it!" she told her fairy friends. "I really like it! This is just what it needed!"

Then Bess hugged Strongjump.
"What a perfect paint day! I knew we
would end up with lots of paint. But I
never thought we'd fix my new
painting, too!"